ecome a star reader with Caillou!

is three-level reading series is designed for pre-readers or
ginning readers and is based on popular Caillou episodes.
e books feature common sight words used with limited grammar.
ich book also offers a set number of target words. These words
e noted in bold print and are presented in a picture dictionary
order to reinforce meaning and expand reading vocabulary.

Level 1
Little Star

For pre-readers to read along
- 125-175 words
- Simple sentences
- Simple vocabulary and common sight words
- Picture dictionary teaching 6 target words

Level 2
Rising Star

For beginning readers to read with support
- 175-250 words
- Longer sentences
- Limited vocabulary and more sight words
- Picture dictionary teaching 8 target words

Level 3
Super Star

For improving readers to read on their own or with support
- 250-350 words
- Longer sentences and more complex grammar
- Varied vocabulary and less-common sight words
- Picture dictionary teaching 10 target words

Text: adaptation by Rebecca Klevberg Moeller
All rights reserved.
Original story written by Sarah Margaret Johanson, based on the animated series CAILLOU
Illustrations: Eric Sévigny, based on the animated series CAILLOU

The PBS KIDS logo is a registered mark of PBS and is used with permission.

Chouette Publishing would like to thank the Government of Canada and SODEC
for their financial support.

Books
Tax Credit

Gestion
SODEC

Bibliothèque et Archives nationales du Québec and Library and Archives
Canada cataloguing in publication

Moeller, Rebecca Klevberg
Caillou: A Special Friend

(Read with Caillou. Level 3)

Previously published as: My imaginary friend.

For children aged 3 and up.

ISBN 978-2-89718-473-5 (softcover)

1. Caillou (Fictitious character) - Juvenile fiction. 2. Imaginary companions -
Juvenile fiction. 3. Friendship - Juvenile fiction. I. Sévigny, Éric. II. Johanson,
Sarah Margaret, 1968-   . My imaginary friend. III. Title.

PS8626.O432C34 2018   jC813'.6   C2017-942124-7
PS9626.O432C34 2018

Printed in Canada
10 9 8 7 6 5 4 3 2 1   CHO2029 MAR2018

MIX
Paper from
responsible sources
FSC® C103304
www.fsc.org

Super Star

Level 3

A Special Friend

Text: Rebecca Klevberg Moeller, Language Teaching Expert
Illustrations: Eric Sévigny, based on the animated series

Caillou is playing **outside**.
He is playing with George.

George is Caillou's special **friend**.

Only Caillou can **see** George.
Mommy can't **see** George.

Grandma can't **see** George.
That makes George special.

Caillou loves **running** with George. "Let's **run** to that **barrel**!" says Caillou.

Caillou **runs** across the **grass**.
He is fast.

Caillou touches the **barrel**.
"I'm the fastest!" he shouts.

Oh no, Mommy's **flowers**!
They're falling.

Oops, Mommy's **flowers** are on the **grass**!

Rosie calls. Time for **lunch**.
Caillou goes to the **house**.

Everyone is having **lunch**.
"Can George eat, too?" Caillou
asks.

Mommy smiles. "Okay."
Caillou finds George a **chair**.

Caillou talks about George.
"George can **run** fast. But I can
run faster."

"Where does George live?"
Grandma asks.
"In our **house**," says Caillou.

Caillou tells more. "George is my best **friend**. He is very special and ..."

"Caillou, your **lunch** is getting cold," Mommy says. "Can George wait **outside**, please?"

Caillou pulls on George's **chair**.
"Please wait **outside**, George."
Mommy thanks George.

After **lunch**, Caillou plays
outside again.
Then Daddy calls Caillou.

Uh-oh, Daddy is by the **barrel**.
He is not happy.

Daddy points to Mommy's **flowers**.
"Who did that?" he asks.

"Um … George did it."
"George?" Daddy asks.
"Your special **friend**?"
"Yes. He didn't mean to."

"Really?" Daddy asks.
"No," says Caillou. "I knocked
the **flowers** off."

Caillou looks down. "I'm sorry.
I didn't mean to."
"That's okay," Daddy says.
"Now, let's clean up!"

"Okay," Caillou says. "And George wants to help, too." "He does?" Daddy laughs. "Yes," says Caillou. "George really is a special **friend**!"

Picture Dictionary

outside

friends

see

run/running

grass

barrel

lunch

flowers

chair

house